In this story, the animals are going on a nature walk in the woods, just like Dr KittyCat reader, Cole, who told us about his experiences and why he enjoyed the story:

'We went to the forest school on a school trip. There's plants and things that are dangerous, and we can't touch them, but someone always does! They get itchy and told off by the teacher, but nobody has needed to go to hospital yet. Someone at school has a pen like the one in the book. It's kind of clever that the animals do the same kind of things we do. I like it—it's good even though it doesn't have dinosaurs or monsters. Can I read the next one, too?'

Cole, age 7

For Huff and Puff, the
bearded dragons – J.C.

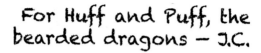

OXFORD
UNIVERSITY PRESS

Great Clarendon Street, Oxford OX2 6DP
Oxford University Press is a department of the University of Oxford.
It furthers the University's objective of excellence in research, scholarship,
and education by publishing worldwide

Oxford is a registered trade mark of Oxford University Press
in the UK and in certain other countries

Text © Jane Clarke and Oxford University Press 2018
Illustrations © Oxford University Press 2018

Cover artwork: Richard Byrne
Cover photograph: Happy monkey/Shutterstock.com
Inside artwork: Dynamo
All animal images from Shutterstock
With thanks to Christopher Tancock for advising on the first aid

The moral rights of the author/illustrator have been asserted

Database right Oxford University Press (maker)

First published in 2018

British Library Cataloguing in Publication Data

Data available

ISBN: 978-0-19-276600-7 (paperback)

2 4 6 8 10 9 7 5 3 1

Printed in China
Paper used in the production of this book is a natural,
recyclable product made from wood grown in sustainable forests.
The manufacturing process conforms to the environmental
regulations of the country of origin.

Are you crazy about your pet?

Do you love cute and cuddly animals?

For budding doctors and nurses!

'I loved the really cute characters and the funny story.'
Poppy, age 5

Perfect for fans of Holly Webb.

'It was very good. I especially liked Logan the puppy. He is so cute.'
Coralie, age 9

'My favourite character was Ginger the kitten with her poorly paw. I really liked the vanbulance.'
Poppy, age 5

'I like Dr KittyCat because she helps the other animals to feel better.'
India, age 5

A note from the author:

Jane says . . .

My dog, Amber, once started sneezing so hard that she couldn't see where she was going, and she started bumping into the furniture. She was allergic to the carpet cleaner I was using, so I had to open all the doors and windows and never use that type of cleaner again!

Dr KittyCat

is ready to rescue

Ginger the Kitten

Jane Clarke

OXFORD
UNIVERSITY PRESS

Chapter One

It was a beautiful sunny day in
Thistletown. Peanut threw open the
door of Dr KittyCat's clinic and sniffed
the fresh spring air. Atchoo-choo, choo!
he sneezed.

Three little animals were waiting
outside for him to let them in. Clover
the bunny and Nutmeg the guinea pig

were snuffling into soggy tissues. Ginger
the kitten was dabbing a fresher-looking
tissue at one red and watery eye.

'Thank you for coming to my
special allergy testing session,' Dr
KittyCat welcomed them. 'It's a good
time of year to find out what is causing
your symptoms and try to do something

about them.'

Atchoo! Peanut sneezed in agreement.

'It's a simple scratch test,' Dr KittyCat went on, 'so it has to be done on bare skin . . .' She washed her paws and took an electric razor out of a drawer.

Atchoo!

'Eek-atchoo!' Peanut squeaked. 'I don't want to be shaved bare and be scratched all over!'

'Don't panic, Peanut,' Dr KittyCat meowed. 'The scratches will be tiny and—'

'If you were bare all over,' Ginger the kitten interrupted, 'Dr KittyCat would knit you a onesie to cover you up!'

Peanut shuddered. Dr KittyCat was a wonderful, kind, and caring furry first-aider, but he wasn't a big fan of her knitting. The woolly pyjamas she'd made when he was poorly had been very itchy, even on top of fur.

'I have to shave only a small area on your arm or your back,' Dr KittyCat reassured him. 'It will soon grow again. Peanut, you'll go first, won't you?'

Peanut stifled another eek and held out his arm. *It's important to be calm to reassure everyone*, Peanut told himself as Dr KittyCat gently shaved a small bare patch.

'It feels a bit tickly. That's all,' he told the others.

Dr KittyCat shaved a similar patch on Nutmeg's, Clover's, and Ginger's arm. They all watched curiously as Dr KittyCat took a marker pen and wrote the numbers 1 to 6 in a grid on Peanut's skin. Then she washed her paws again and took six small droplet bottles from her medical cabinet.

'Each of these bottles contains an extract from something you might be allergic to,' she explained. 'I'll put a droplet on your skin next to a number so I know which extract it is.' Dr KittyCat squeezed a drop out of the first bottle on

to Peanut's arm next to the number 1.
Then she took a fresh, sterilized needle
from a pack. Peanut closed his eyes
tightly and tried to think of cheese.

'Next, I scratch the skin through the droplet so it goes into the skin,' Dr KittyCat explained as she demonstrated on Peanut.

'Did it hurt?' asked Nutmeg.

Peanut opened his eyes. 'It's a bit sharp, but it isn't painful,' he squeaked. He felt very brave as he watched Dr KittyCat repeat the process with the other five droplet bottles. She took a new needle each time, he noticed, and disposed of the old ones in a special bin.

'Well done, Peanut. You're an excellent patient,' Dr KittyCat told him. 'Now we have to wait at least fifteen minutes to see if there's any swelling or redness at the scratch sites.'

Soon Peanut, Ginger, Nutmeg, and Clover had all had their scratch tests. Peanut checked the clinic clock.

It seemed to be moving very slowly. The other little animals were staring anxiously at it, too. *The best thing to do*, Peanut thought, *is to talk about something else while we wait for our results.*

'Are any of you going on Mrs Hazelnut's walk this afternoon?' he asked.

'I am,' said Ginger. 'It's a nature spotter walk. I'm good at nature—I know what lots of things are. I shall spot everything!'

'I don't know everything,' piped up Clover, 'but I've learned a lot since our camping trip.'

'So have I!' said Nutmeg. 'What

about you, Peanut?'

'I'm not so good at knowing the names of countryside things,' Peanut admitted. 'I grew up in the town.'

'Then you should go on the nature spotter walk, too!' Dr KittyCat told him. She looked at the clock. 'But first it's time to check the results of the scratch test!'

Chapter Two

Peanut stared at his arm. 'There's a bump next to number 4,' he squeaked. 'It's a bit itchy.'

'I have a red mark next to number 2,' Nutmeg whistled.

'Me too!' said Clover. 'What does it mean, Dr KittyCat?'

Dr KittyCat carefully examined the

scratch sites on the little animals' arms.

'It's good news,' Dr KittyCat meowed. 'None of you is dangerously allergic to anything I tested. Number 2 was tree pollen—which means Clover's and Nutmeg's runny noses are the result of being sensitive to that.'

'What's number 4?' asked Peanut. 'It isn't cheese, is it?!'

'Don't panic, Peanut,' Dr KittyCat smiled. 'Number 5 was cheese and dairy produce, and there's no reaction to that on your arm.

And number 6 was nuts, so you're fine with them, too. Number 4 was flower pollen.'

'Eek! There are flowers everywhere!' Peanut squeaked.

'Yes, tree and flower pollens are hard to avoid at this time of year unless you stay inside,' Dr KittyCat said. 'I've noticed you're all sneezing and snuffling less now you are inside the clinic than you did when you first came in.'

The little animals looked at one another.

'Does that mean we have to miss Mrs Hazelnut's nature walk?' Clover asked.

'None of you has a serious allergy,' Dr KittyCat reassured them. 'Peanut, you're old enough for me to prescribe special tablets called antihistamines to take once a day, and so is Nutmeg. The tablets will help dry up your snuffles and make your eyes less itchy so you can enjoy the walk.'

Peanut was puzzled. *'Anti' means 'against'*, he thought. *I need anti-flower pollen!* Aloud he asked, 'What is histamine?'

'Your body sees things you are allergic or sensitive to as a threat to it,' Dr KittyCat explained. 'So your body's defence system, called the immune system, makes a chemical called histamine. Histamine causes fluid to build up—so your skin swells up, or you sneeze or your eyes water.'

'Histamine doesn't sound very useful,' Peanut commented.

'It is if you are bitten or stung by something poisonous,' Dr KittyCat told him. 'It can help rid your body of the poison. But you're right, the body often gets it wrong and thinks something is a threat when it shouldn't be.'

Dr KittyCat opened her medicine cupboard and took down two packets of antihistamine tablets. 'Take one tablet right away,' she told Peanut and

Nutmeg. 'Then, from tomorrow on, during the allergy season, you should take one every morning when you wake up.'

Peanut fetched glasses of water so they could each swallow an antihistamine tablet.

'What about me?' asked Clover.

'You're a bit too young to take the tablets,' Dr KittyCat told the little bunny, 'but you'd look cute in sunglasses, and they would protect your eyes from pollen.'

She reached for a little medicine pot. 'This is petroleum jelly,' she told Clover as she gently rubbed it around the bunny's nostrils.

'It will help stop pollen getting into your nose.'

'And me?' mewed Ginger, dabbing at her eye.

'You have the all-clear,' Dr KittyCat told her with a smile. 'You don't need to take antihistamine tablets because you're not sensitive to any of the things I tested.'

'So why does Ginger's eye look red and watery?' Peanut asked. 'Could she be allergic to something that you didn't test for?'

'That's possible,' Dr KittyCat said. 'You can be allergic to practically anything! But only one of Ginger's eyes is sore, so I will check that before I think about doing any other allergy tests.' Dr KittyCat took the ophthalmoscope out of her flowery doctor's bag.

'Does your eye itch?' she asked the little kitten.

Ginger shook her head.

'Keep still now, Ginger.' Dr

KittyCat shone the special light into Ginger's eye and carefully examined it.

'Well done, Ginger,' Dr KittyCat murmured. 'You don't have an eye infection. Your eye is sore because you have a very slight scratch on the iris . . .'

'The iris?
That's a flower,
isn't it? They make me
sneeze!' Peanut groaned.

'The iris is the name for the
coloured part of your eye, as well as a
flower,' Dr KittyCat explained. 'I think
you must have poked your eye with
something, Ginger.'

Ginger frowned. 'I don't
remember,' she said. 'But I was chasing
a butterfly this morning, and I ran
through a bush . . .'

'Maybe a leaf or a little twig went
in your eye,' Dr KittyCat said. 'It's out
now, so there's no need to worry.'

She turned to the
little animals.

'You all have
sore or itchy eyes, so
I think it's a good idea
if I give you all eye drops.
They will make you feel better straight
away.'

Peanut and the little animals tilted
their heads back so that Dr KittyCat
could gently squeeze the cool, soothing
drops into their eyes.

'That feels good,' sighed Peanut.

'Well done, everyone,' Dr KittyCat
purred. 'You've all been purr-fect
patients, so you all deserve a sticker.'

I was a purr-fect patient for Dr KittyCat!

'Will we see you later on the nature walk, Peanut?' Ginger asked as the little animals left the clinic, proudly wearing their stickers. 'It starts at two o'clock at the nature hut.'

'I'll be there if I have time!' Peanut waved Ginger goodbye and sat down at his desk and opened the *Furry First-aid Book*. He took out his pencil and scratched his ear with it. There were an awful lot of things to write in the book. Scratch tests, allergens, immune system, histamine, antihistamines, eye drops. It was very complicated for a

small mouse and a lot to write down . . .
Would he be finished by two o'clock?

Chapter Three

It's almost two o'clock. I'll take my notes with me and finish them on the walk, Peanut thought. He picked up the heavy *Furry First-aid Book* and walked across the meadow behind the clinic.

Mrs Hazelnut and a group of little animals were standing outside the nature hut. Everyone was holding

clipboards and pencils.

'We're just about to set off, Peanut,'
Mrs Hazelnut greeted him. 'You can
choose which nature checklist you want
to do. Trees, plants, flowers, fungi, bugs,
or butterflies. How about the flower
sheet?' Without waiting for a reply,

she fixed a flower spotter sheet on a clipboard and thrust it into Peanut's paws.

'My paws aren't big enough to hold a book, a pencil, and a clipboard,' Peanut squeaked in alarm. He didn't want to drop the *Furry First-aid Book*.

Mrs Hazelnut caught the clipboard as it slipped towards the ground.

'I don't need a clipboard, thanks. I'll just help the others,' Peanut told her. 'That way, I'll learn about everything!'

'Come on, then!' Mrs Hazelnut set off briskly down the path that led along the side of the meadow and into the wood. Willow the duckling stopped to nibble at a leafy green plant.

'What are you doing?' Peanut asked the fluffy duckling. Willow showed him her plant spotter checklist. She took her pencil and put a smiley face next to a picture labelled goosegrass.

'I'm checking which plants taste nice!' she said. 'Fresh green plants and berries are yummy!'

'Eek! Shouldn't you check if a plant is poisonous first?' Peanut squeaked. 'You could make yourself very poorly.'

'Don't panic, Peanut,' Willow told him. 'Mrs Hazelnut gave us a safety talk. And look, this sheet clearly marks the poisonous plants.'

Peanut studied the sheet. There were big circles with red crosses over two plants. One of them had berries, and the other had spiky leaves. Peanut stared at the plants in the hedge.

'There are so many different sorts!' he murmured. 'It's hard to be sure which one is which . . .'

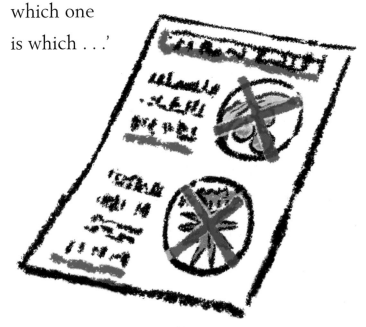

'If I'm not sure of anything, I won't try it,' Willow reassured him. 'I already know a lot about plants. You don't need to worry about me. Go and check on Posy and Logan. I'm not sure they know what they're doing.'

She pointed along the path. Posy and Logan were standing under a tree snuffling at something.

Peanut hurried up to them. They were sniffing suspiciously at a big mushroom with red spots on it.

'Don't lick it!' Peanut squeaked.

'We're not that silly!' Posy woofed. She held out the fungi spotter sheet for Peanut to see. There was a big red warning at the top of it. DO NOT TOUCH FUNGI (EVEN WITH YOUR NOSE)!

'You missed
Mrs Hazelnut's
safety talk,' Logan
said excitedly.
'She told us only
experts should identify mushrooms
and toadstools. She made us promise
not to touch any of them just in case.
Some mushrooms are tasty, but some of
them are so poisonous that just a few
mouthfuls could kill you! They're really
interesting. Posy and I are working
together on the checklist.'

Peanut's mouth dropped open.
'You're right to take care,' he squeaked.

He went to check on what Ginger

was doing. She was standing beside a bush with bright yellow flowers and sharp spikes, ticking something off on her checklist.

'What did you choose?' Peanut asked her, dodging out of the way of a bee that was buzzing towards a flower.

Ginger showed him
her butterfly spotter
sheet.

'Insects seem to like these
bushes,' Peanut commented as a bright
orange, red, and brown
butterfly touched down
beside them.

'Ooh, that's a new
one!' Ginger squealed
excitedly. The butterfly fluttered into
the sky.

'Stop, butterfly!' Ginger meowed as
she chased after it. The butterfly settled
on top of another spiky bush.

Ginger stood on her back legs and

stretched up her front paws to try and catch it.

'Yeee-owl!' she cried as she fell into the bush. The butterfly fluttered off.

'Are you OK?' Peanut asked her.

'I'm fine, thanks!' Ginger picked herself up, brushed her ears with her paws, and made a tick on her sheet. 'I've only got two more butterflies to find . . . There's another one!' She scampered off after a yellow butterfly.

Clover and Nutmeg were staring up into a tree.

'How are you two doing?' Peanut asked. They showed him their tree spotter sheet.

'We're finding out which trees have the most pollen on them so we can avoid them,' Clover explained.

'You're not sneezing now,' Peanut commented. 'Dr KittyCat's antihistamine tablets must be working.'

'They are!' Nutmeg said happily. 'How about you, Peanut? There are a lot of wild flowers around.'

Peanut gingerly sniffed at a rose. Dusty pollen rushed up his nostrils.

Atchoo! he sneezed.

Ginger romped up. 'Maybe you'd better not sniff pollen,' she grinned. 'But I'm not allergic to anything. I've checked off all the butterflies. I'm going to get Mrs Hazelnut's flower sheet and see how many I can sniff!'

Peanut watched her hurry off, shoving her little pink nose into any flower she passed.

I'll finish writing up my notes while everyone's busy, he thought. He settled himself under a tree and opened the

Furry First-aid Book. The notes were almost complete, but he hadn't had time to write about Ginger's eye. He took his pencil and wrote down the name Ginger.

There was a sudden 'YEEOWWWL!' Peanut looked up. Ginger was running around in circles, squealing loudly.

She didn't make a fuss when she fell into the bush, Peanut thought. *She must really be in pain!* He jumped to his feet, ready to rescue.

Chapter Four

Peanut and Mrs Hazelnut rushed up to
Ginger.

'What's wrong?' Mrs Hazelnut
asked anxiously

'Meoww, owww, oww, owww,
owww!' Ginger squealed, jumping up
and down.

'Can you show us where it hurts?'

Peanut asked her.

'Nooo-ooo!' Ginger wailed. She backed away from Peanut and Mrs Hazelnut. 'It hurts! It hurts!' she shrieked.

'We can't help if you don't stand still,' Peanut squeaked.

But Ginger started running around in circles again, mewing loudly.

'This is an emergency!' Peanut whispered to Mrs Hazelnut. 'We need Dr KittyCat!'

Mrs Hazelnut nodded. 'There's a phone in the nature hut,' she said. 'You go and call her. I'll stay here and try to calm Ginger down.'

'I'm on my way!' Peanut raced back to the hut and grabbed the emergency telephone. He heard the phone ring twice, and Dr KittyCat answered.

'Dr KittyCat's clinic. How can I help?'

'Come qu—qu—
quick!' Peanut panted.
'Please take a deep
breath and tell me your
name, where you are, and
what has happened,' Dr
KittyCat said calmly.

'It's Peanut, your assistant!'
Peanut gabbled. 'I'm at the nature
hut. Ginger's out on the nature walk.
Something's happened. She's in pain!'

'Try not to panic, Peanut,' Dr
KittyCat replied calmly. 'Has Ginger
collapsed? Is she bleeding or having
trouble breathing?'

'N—n—no,' Peanut squeaked.

'That's good,' Dr KittyCat murmured. 'Is someone with her?'

Peanut took a deep breath.

'Mrs Hazelnut is with her. But Ginger's hurting so badly she can't keep still. We need you!'

'Keep everyone calm,' Dr KittyCat purred. 'The vanbulance is ready. I'll be there in a whisker. If you're sure she hasn't broken anything, it would help if

you could get Ginger to the hut. I can't
drive the vanbulance down the nature
walk path.'

'I'll do my best!' Peanut said. He
put down the phone and raced back to
where he'd left Ginger.

She was lying face down on the grass,
mewing pitifully. Her front paws were
clamped over her nose. Mrs Hazelnut

was kneeling beside her, and the other little animals were gathered around, looking concerned.

'Dr KittyCat's on her way!' Peanut panted.

'I think Ginger's hurt her nose,' Mrs Hazelnut whispered in his ear. 'But I can't get her to take her paws away from her face so I can look at it.'

'Dr KittyCat will know what to do,' Peanut said. 'She asked us to get Ginger to the nature hut if we are sure she hasn't broken a bone.'

'She's only just stopped running around,' Mrs Hazelnut said. 'I don't think she can have a fracture.'

Peanut thought hard about the questions Dr KittyCat might ask. 'Ginger, did you fall, or trip, or bang your head, or twist your neck, or catch your tail in anything?' he asked the poorly kitten. 'Or did anything drop off a tree and hit you?'

'No, no, no, no, no, noo-ooo!' Ginger squealed from behind her paws. 'Id's by dose!'

'Nothing's happened that might fracture a bone,' Peanut confirmed. 'Ginger's safe to move.'

'We'll have to carry her.' Mrs Hazelnut thought for a moment. Then she pulled two long sticks out of the

hedge. She took off her cardigan and
pushed the sticks through the sleeves.

'I made a stretcher!' she told the
little animals who were watching open-
mouthed. 'Help me get Ginger on to it.
That's it!'

'Now let's all carry the stretcher together.' Peanut took one of the sticks in his paw.

'One, two, three, lift!' said Mrs Hazelnut.

They carried the sobbing kitten into the nature hut and carefully set down the stretcher. Mrs Hazelnut stood back. She looked unsure about what to do next.

Mrs Hazelnut is an amazing organizer, thought Peanut. *But she's not a first-aider, and I am. It's my job to reassure the patient . . .*

He scurried up so he could whisper in the poorly kitten's furry ear. 'Well done, Ginger. Dr KittyCat will be here soon to examine your nose. Can you take your paws away so she can see?'

'Meowwww, meowww,' Ginger mewed as she slowly let her paws sink to her side.

Peanut stifled a gasp. The tip of Ginger's little pink nose had swollen up to twice its normal size, and there was a big red mark in the middle.

Eek! Peanut thought. *Ginger must be allergic to something!* He took a deep breath. *It's very important not to panic the patient,* he remembered. *I must pretend to be calm, even if I don't feel it.*

'Dr KittyCat will be here in a whisker,' he whispered in Ginger's ear. 'You'll be safe in her paws.'

Inside, Peanut was panicking. He hadn't had time to check Dr KittyCat's bag. Would she remember it? Would she have everything she needed to treat Ginger and make her better?

All of a sudden, he heard the nee-nah, nee-nah, nee-nah of an emergency siren getting closer and closer. There was a screee-eeech of tyres, and the siren stopped. A camper van painted with bright flowers was outside the hut. Peanut sighed with relief.

'The vanbulance has arrived,' he told everyone. 'Dr KittyCat is here!'

Chapter Five

Dr KittyCat slid open the vanbulance door and swished her tail out of the way as she climbed down from the driver's seat. Peanut was glad to see she was clutching her flowery doctor's bag in one silvery paw. He raced outside to meet her.

'The tip of Ginger's nose is swelling

up,' he told her as they hurried into the nature hut.

'So it is.' Dr KittyCat knelt down beside the sobbing kitten. 'It will be all right, Ginger,' she purred reassuringly. 'I'll find out what's wrong and make it better. Do you hurt anywhere else?'

'No-ooo,' Ginger moaned. She gave a little hiccup and stopped sobbing.

'You're being very brave,' Dr KittyCat smiled. 'First, I need to check your airway . . .'

I wish I could be as calm as Dr KittyCat! Peanut thought as he watched her look in Ginger's mouth, then carefully listen to Ginger's chest with her stethoscope.

'Your breathing is fine,' Dr KittyCat smiled at Ginger. 'And so is your heart rate. I'm going to check your blood pressure now.' She slipped a small rubber cuff on to Ginger's arm and inflated it. The cuff was attached to a monitor dial. Dr KittyCat looked at the numbers and smiled.

'That's good,' she purred. 'Your eye is looking better, too. So the only problem is the tip of your nose . . .'

'It hurts!' Ginger wailed. Tears spurted from her eyes.

'I know,' Dr KittyCat murmured, holding Ginger's paw. 'I will make it stop hurting as fast as I can. Peanut, please hand me the magnifying glass so I can take a good look.'

Peanut opened Dr KittyCat's bag and pushed aside her knitting. *I think everything's in here,* he thought with relief as he searched through the contents. He handed over the magnifying glass.

'I can see exactly what's causing the problem,' Dr KittyCat said, handing the magnifying glass to Peanut so he could take a look.

In the middle of the red spot on the end of Ginger's nose he could see something that looked like a tiny splinter. Only it wasn't a splinter. It was a sting!

'You've been stung by a bee!' Peanut exclaimed.

'Poor Ginger,' Dr KittyCat murmured. 'Bee stings are very painful. We need to get it out. Can you be brave a little bit longer and stay very still for me?'

Ginger blinked in agreement.

Peanut handed Dr KittyCat her medical tweezers.

'Thanks, Peanut. Tweezers are good for splinters, but it's best not to use them for getting out stings,' Dr KittyCat told him. 'They might squeeze the poison that's left in the sting into Ginger's nose.' She thought for a moment. 'Pass me a tongue depressor, please.'

'Why do you need one of these?' Peanut asked as he handed over a long, flat tongue depressor. 'You've already looked down Ginger's throat.'

'You can scrape off a sting with a

flat, bendy surface like this,' Dr KittyCat told him. 'Watch. You start at the place where the sting enters the skin, then gently scrape away from it. Like this . . .'

In less than a minute the sting was out. Dr KittyCat put it, and the tongue depressor, in a clinical waste bag.

'Well done, Ginger!' she meowed. Peanut handed her the paw-cleansing gel and a tube of sting relief cream. Dr KittyCat cleansed her paws then carefully smeared a tiny blob of cream on to Ginger's nose.

'It will take a while for
the swelling to go down,
and for the pain to disappear
completely,' Dr KittyCat told
her. 'But this should make your nose
feel a bit better straight away. If the
pain comes back, an ice pack or a cold
compress will help.'

'Thank you!' Ginger mewed as
she got to her feet. 'I don't feel so bad
now!'

'You've been so brave, you deserve
another sticker!' Dr KittyCat smiled.
Peanut took one out of the bag, and
Ginger stuck it proudly on her collar.
Everyone clapped their paws.

'Make sure you write down that Ginger had a bee sting,' Dr KittyCat whispered to Peanut. 'Each time you get stung, it can get worse.'

Peanut nodded. He knew how important it was to record everything in the *Furry First-aid Book*.

Dr KittyCat stood up and turned to speak to the little animals. 'Fortunately, Ginger isn't allergic to bee stings,' she said, 'and the sting wasn't inside her nose, mouth, or throat, so it didn't affect her breathing. But if any of you ever do get stung in those places, you should get medical help straight away if you find it hard to breathe.'

The little animals nodded.

'And it's a good idea to get checked out if you are stung anywhere more than ten times,' Dr KittyCat added.

'Ten times?' Ginger squealed. 'Once was one time too many!'

'If you are allergic to them, any bee or wasp sting is dangerous,' Dr KittyCat went on. 'If you ever have a bad allergic reaction to anything, you should call for help fast. Doctors have special equipment for that. I keep mine inside the vanbulance.

Would you like to see it?'

A chorus of little voices cried, 'Yes, please!'

Chapter Six

Everyone piled into the vanbulance. They squashed themselves around the table while Dr KittyCat reached into a cubbyhole and took down a box.

It had the words Anaphylaxis Kit written in big letters on it.

Eek! That's a tricky word, Peanut thought. *Anna-fill-axe-sis.* He sounded

it out in his head so he'd remember it
when he wrote up his notes later.

'Anaphylaxis is a special name for a very bad allergic reaction,' Dr KittyCat told them. 'Fortunately, it's quite rare, but it is very serious.'

'Our allergies aren't serious, are they?' Peanut asked anxiously.

'Itchy eyes and runny noses aren't serious symptoms,' Dr KittyCat reassured him. 'Don't panic, Peanut. You and Clover and Nutmeg are just sensitive to certain things. You don't have dangerous allergies that cause anaphylaxis. And Ginger's reaction to the bee sting was just in the area of the sting, so that wasn't an anaphylactic reaction.'

'What are the symptoms of anna . . . anna-fill-axe-sis?' Peanut asked.

'There are many different symptoms to look for, including collapse, skin rashes, difficulties with breathing or swallowing, and sickness,' Dr KittyCat said. 'The whole body goes into shock. It can happen quickly, so if you are worried about someone you must call an ambulance straight away. They will need a special injection. I keep them in here.' Dr Kittycat opened the box. Inside were tubes of different sizes.

'Oooh!' The murmur went around the table. Everyone was watching wide-eyed.

Dr KittyCat took one out and took off the lid. It looked like a fat ballpoint pen with no tip. 'This is an anaphylaxis pen,' she told the little animals. 'If

someone has anaphylaxis, you have to push it firmly into their thigh so it squirts out a dose of medicine to help them breathe.'

'Wheeee!' Nutmeg whistled. 'That might save someone's life! Have you ever had to use one, Dr KittyCat?'

'No,' Dr KittyCat said, 'but plenty of first-aiders have. If we have a patient who has a dangerous allergy, we give them pens so they can have them with them at all times.'

'Why are the pens different sizes?' asked Posy.

'Because animals come in lots of different sizes,' Dr KittyCat smiled.

'A puppy like you needs a bigger dose than a mouse like Peanut!'

She closed the lid of the box and put it away. 'Don't forget!' she told them. 'Treat any signs of anaphylaxis as an emergency and get the patient to a hospital as soon as possible!'

The little animals nodded seriously.

Peanut noticed Ginger gently touching her nose with her paw.

'How is it feeling now, Ginger?' he asked.

'It's still sore,' Ginger said. 'But I want to go and tick off the other flowers on my list. I don't think I'll sniff them, though!'

Dr KittyCat opened her bag and handed Mrs Hazelnut the sting relief cream. 'You'd better take this, just in case!' she purred.

'That could be useful!' Mrs Hazelnut smiled. 'Let's finish our nature walk,' she told the little animals. 'Thank you for coming to the rescue, Dr KittyCat, and for explaining about allergies.'

'You're welcome!' Dr KittyCat said. Peanut offered to go back to the clinic and climbed into the vanbulance next to Dr KittyCat.

'Ready to roll?' Dr KittyCat asked Peanut.

'Ready to roll!' Peanut confirmed.

It was such a short journey back to the clinic that there was hardly time for Dr KittyCat's driving to make Peanut feel nervous. As soon as they'd screeched to a halt, Peanut opened his eyes to check the *Furry First-aid Book* hadn't rolled off the seat beside him. He still had Ginger's notes to write up, and there were lots more things to write about now!

Inside the clinic, Dr KittyCat pulled her chair into a beam of spring sunshine that was shining through the window. She settled in it with a happy sigh.

'I'll have a catnap before I finish my knitting,' she purred.

Peanut looked up from his notes. 'What are you making?' he asked nervously. *I think I might be a tiny bit allergic to Dr KittyCat's knitting*, he thought.

'Take a look in my bag,' Dr KittyCat told him.

'That reminds me. I need to replace the tube of sting relief cream and check

that everything's in there,'
Peanut said. 'I'll do it now.'
He fetched his little ladder
from the corner and
rolled it over to the
medical cabinet so
he could reach
a new tube of
cream.

Then he scampered over to open
Dr KittyCat's flowery doctor's bag.

'Sting relief cream,
ophthalmoscope, magnifying
glass, tweezers, tongue depressors,
stethoscope, thermometer, scissors,
syringes, surgical headlamp, dental
mirror,' he murmured. 'Paw-cleansing
gel, wipes, bandages, tape, cotton
gauze, sticking plasters, instant cool
packs, peppermint lozenges, medicines,
ointments, reward stickers . . . and
knitting!'

He pulled out something that
looked like a knitted paper bag and
held it up.

'It's for you, Peanut,' Dr KittyCat smiled sleepily. 'I just need to finish the shoulder strap. I thought it might be useful if you had your own little bag to carry the *Furry First-aid Book* in.'

Peanut gave a happy little squeak. 'That's really useful. If I'd had that bag on the nature walk, I could have carried the book, the pencil, and the clipboard. Thank you, Dr KittyCat!'

Dr KittyCat had knitted him something he liked. Peanut grinned from ear to ear. He couldn't wait to use his new bag!

The end

Dr KittyCat's top ten tips for staying healthy and safe on a nature walk (with a grown-up, of course):

1. Never eat any part of a plant or fungus.

2. Do not drink water from streams.

3. If you're taking a picnic, wash your hands, or use wipes, before you eat anything.

4. Make sure you know what stinging nettles and brambles look like, so that you can take care around them and avoid stings or scratches.

5. Walk carefully, remembering that paths can be slippery, and look out for fallen branches or other obstacles. Only climb trees if you have permission from a grown-up and listen carefully to any instructions.

6. Pack a basic first-aid kit for your walk.

7. It's useful to carry insect repellent.

8. Take sun hats and sun cream.

9. Make sure you have plenty of water.

10. If you get caught in an unexpected thunderstorm, shelter under a clump of low trees and away from metal objects. Don't stand under tall trees as these are more likely to attract lightning.

If you loved Ginger the Kitten, here's an extract from another Dr KittyCat adventure:

Dr KittyCat is ready to rescue: Peanut the Mouse

In this story, it's Dr KittyCat's assistant Peanut who's poorly. It turns out he's rather a panicky patient, but he feels safe in Dr KittyCat's paws.

'Your temperature is higher than it should be . . .' Dr KittyCat murmured. 'Does anything hurt, Peanut?'

Peanut tried to sit up. He felt very dizzy, and he felt sore all over, from the whiskers on his nose to the tip of his tail.

'I ache!' he squeaked. 'And my throat hurts.'

'That's because your body is fighting some kind of infection,' Dr KittyCat told him.

'What kind of infection?' Peanut whimpered.

Here are some other stories that we think you'll love!

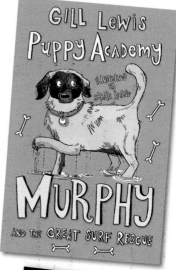